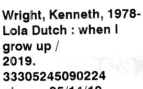

Lola Dutch
When I Grow Up

KENNETH

AND SARAH JANE WRIGHT

BLOOMSBURY
CHILDREN'S BOOKS
NEW YORK LONDON OXFORD NEW DELHI SYDNEY

This is Lola. Lola Dutch.

Lola Dutch wants to be too much.

"Bear! We have an emergency!" said Lola. "I
don't know what I want to be when I grow up!"
"That is a big decision. Should we discuss it
over tea?" asked Bear.

"Oh, there's no time for that," said Lola.
"Quick, to the den!"

Bear's den was the perfect place to find inspiration. There were fascinating books on biology, astronomy, and history, but today one particular book caught Lola's eye.

"That's it! I'm destined for the stage," said Lola.
"Forward, friends! We must rehearse!"

Gator built the set.

Pig composed the orchestrations.

Crane designed the costumes.

"Lola Dutch, I loved it so much!" said Bear.

"Thank you, Bear. But actually . . ."

"... I might want to be an inventor
when I grow up," said Lola.

Lola knew that to be an inventor she must . . .

Research,

Experiment,

Improvise . . .

Hypothesize,

OOPS!

and Discover!
Lola's imagination . . .

. . . soared!

"Lola Dutch, you have learned so much," said Bear.

"But what if I'm supposed to be something else when I grow up?" Lola wondered. She took a deep breath and looked around.

Lola noticed the hum of the bees
and the fragrance of the flowers.

"Maybe I could be a botanist!" she said.

In the greenhouse . . .

Gator prepped the soil.

Pig planted the seeds.

Crane watered the seedlings.

"Bear, that's it! I will make
the earth laugh with flowers!"
Lola's ideas . . .

"Lola Dutch, you've grown so much," said Bear.

"But Bear, I still can't decide what I want to be!
Maybe what I REALLY want to be is . . ."

"...a judge in the highest court."

"Or maybe an Egyptologist."

"Or an astronaut,

a pastry chef,

a veterinarian,

a safari ranger,

a yoga instructor,

or a chemist?"

"But I can't decide.

It's ALL TOO MUCH!"

said Lola Dutch.

"Lola, what do you want to be right now?" asked Bear.

"I just want to be a kid and learn about everything!" said Lola.

"Well then," said Bear, "I think you *should*
be a kid and learn about everything."

"Oh, Bear, you always know just what to say."

"I still have a little time before
I grow up, right?" asked Lola.
"Absolutely," said Bear.

"Good," said Lola, "because I have a
few more things I'd like to be tomorrow."

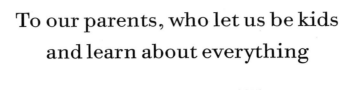

To our parents, who let us be kids
and learn about everything

BLOOMSBURY CHILDREN'S BOOKS
Bloomsbury Publishing Inc., part of Bloomsbury Publishing Plc
1385 Broadway, New York, NY 10018

BLOOMSBURY, BLOOMSBURY CHILDREN'S BOOKS, and the Diana logo are trademarks of Bloomsbury Publishing Plc

First published in the United States of America in January 2019 by Bloomsbury Children's Books

Bloomsbury books may be purchased for business or promotional use. For information on bulk purchases
please contact Macmillan Corporate and Premium Sales Department at specialmarkets@macmillan.com

Library of Congress Cataloging-in-Publication Data
Names: Wright, Kenneth, author. | Wright, Sarah Jane, illustrator.
Title: Lola Dutch when I grow up / by Kenneth Wright ; illustrated by Sarah Jane Wright.
Description: New York : Bloomsbury, 2019.
Summary: Determined to decide what to be when she grows up, Lola tries several careers
before listening to her friend Bear, who reminds her that she need not be in a hurry.
Identifiers: LCCN 2018011660 (print) • LCCN 2018018258 (e-book)
ISBN 978-1-68119-554-4 (hardcover) • ISBN 978-1-68119-555-1 (e-book) • ISBN 978-1-68119-556-8 (e-PDF)
Subjects: | CYAC: Occupations–Fiction. | Enthusiasm–Fiction. | Friendship–Fiction. | Animals–Fiction.
Classification: LCC PZ7.1.W79 Lq 2019 (print) | LCC PZ7.1.W79 (e-book) | DDC [E]–dc23
LC record available at https://lccn.loc.gov/2018011660

Art created with pencil, gouache, and watercolor
Typeset in Bodoni Six ITC Std
Book design by Donna Mark and Jeanette Levy
Printed in China by Leo Paper Products, Heshan, Guangdong
2 4 6 8 10 9 7 5 3 1

All papers used by Bloomsbury Publishing Plc are natural, recyclable products made from wood grown in well-managed
forests. The manufacturing processes conform to the environmental regulations of the country of origin.

To find out more about our authors and books visit www.bloomsbury.com and sign up for our newsletters.

Research some of the places, characters, and creators who inspired Lola Dutch: The Paris Opera House
(also featured on the reverse of the jacket), completed 1875, designed by Charles Garnier (1825–1898) •
Brünnhilde, the Valkyrie from Richard Wagner's (1813–1883) *The Ring of the Nibelung* (1876) •
Leonardo da Vinci (1452–1519), artist, inventor, and mathematician • Orville Wright (1871–1948)
and Wilbur Wright (1867–1912) used the lift equation (wright.nasa.gov) when they invented
and built the world's first successful airplane • The reference to "Earth laughs in flowers"
is from the poem "Hamatreya" (1846) by Ralph Waldo Emerson (1803–1882),
essayist and poet • Carrousel La Belle Époque, Place de l'Hôtel de Ville, Paris •
Sandra Day O'Connor (b. 1930), the first woman to serve on the
Supreme Court of the United States • The Great Sphinx and
Pyramids (c. 2575–c. 2465 BCE), Giza, Egypt.